David McKee

ELMER
and the
PATCHWORK STORY

This Elmer book belongs to:

....

I am a reader and I celebrated World Book Day 2024 with this gift from my local bookseller and Andersen Press.

WORLD BOOK DAY®

World Book Day's mission is to offer every child and young person the opportunity to read and love books by giving you the chance to have a book of your own. To find out more, and for fun activities including video stories, audiobooks and book recommendations, visit worldbookday.com
World Book Day is a charity sponsored by National Book Tokens.

World Book Day® and the associated logo are the registered trademarks of World Book Day® Limited.
Registered charity number 1079257 (England a...
Registered company number 03783095 (...

Andersen Press

Elmer was walking his evening walk with Rose when they spotted Aunt Zelda.

"Hello, dears," said Zelda. "The baby elephants want to hear their favourite story, but I can't remember how it goes."

"The one about the magic biscuit!" said a baby elephant.

"I don't know that one," said Rose.

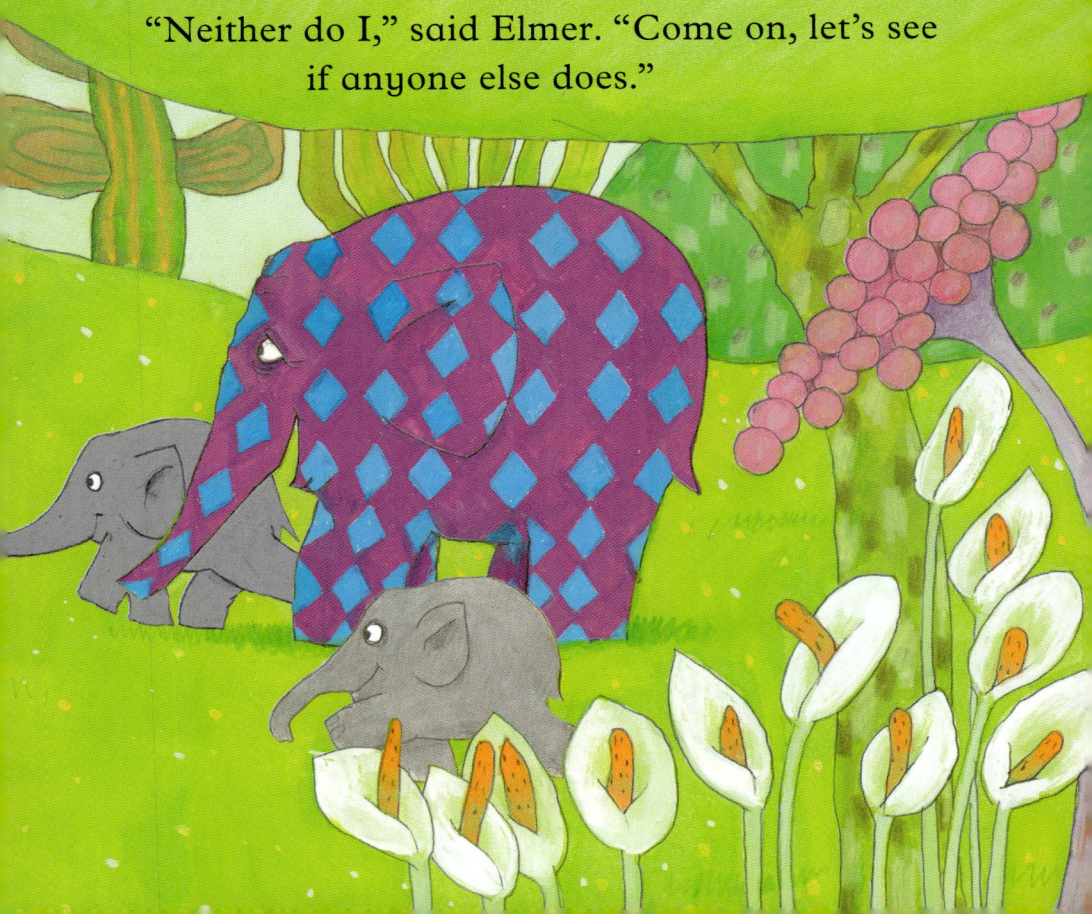

"Neither do I," said Elmer. "Come on, let's see if anyone else does."

Their walk took them past the river.
"Good evening," said a hippo.
"Hello, Hippo," said Elmer. "Have you heard of the story about the magic biscuit?"
"I don't think so," said Hippo. "But the best stories are set somewhere nice, like a lake."
"Cake, dear?" asked Zelda. "No, it's a biscuit."

Next, they saw the monkeys.
"Hello, Monkey," said Elmer, "you might be able to help. Do you know the story about the magic biscuit?"
"Probably," said Monkey thoughtfully. "Is the main character a monkey? Stories with monkeys in them are my favourite."
"Maybe," said Elmer.

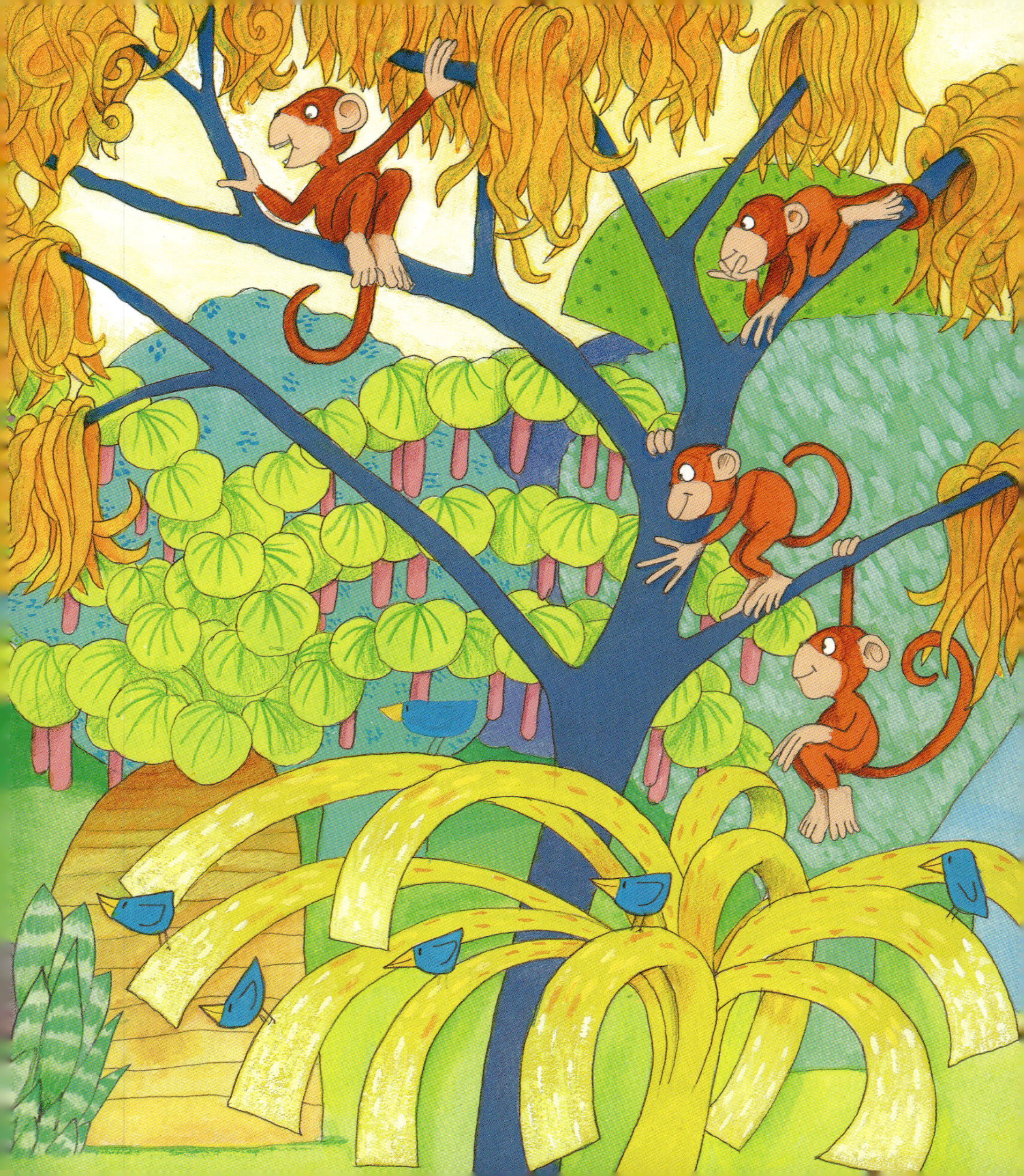

Soon after, they met Tiger.

"Hello, Tiger," called Rose. "We can't remember how the story about the magic biscuit goes. Can you help?"

"Hmm," thought Tiger. "Is that the one where the biscuit keeps disappearing?"

"I don't think a disappearing biscuit is much of a mystery . . ." said Zelda.

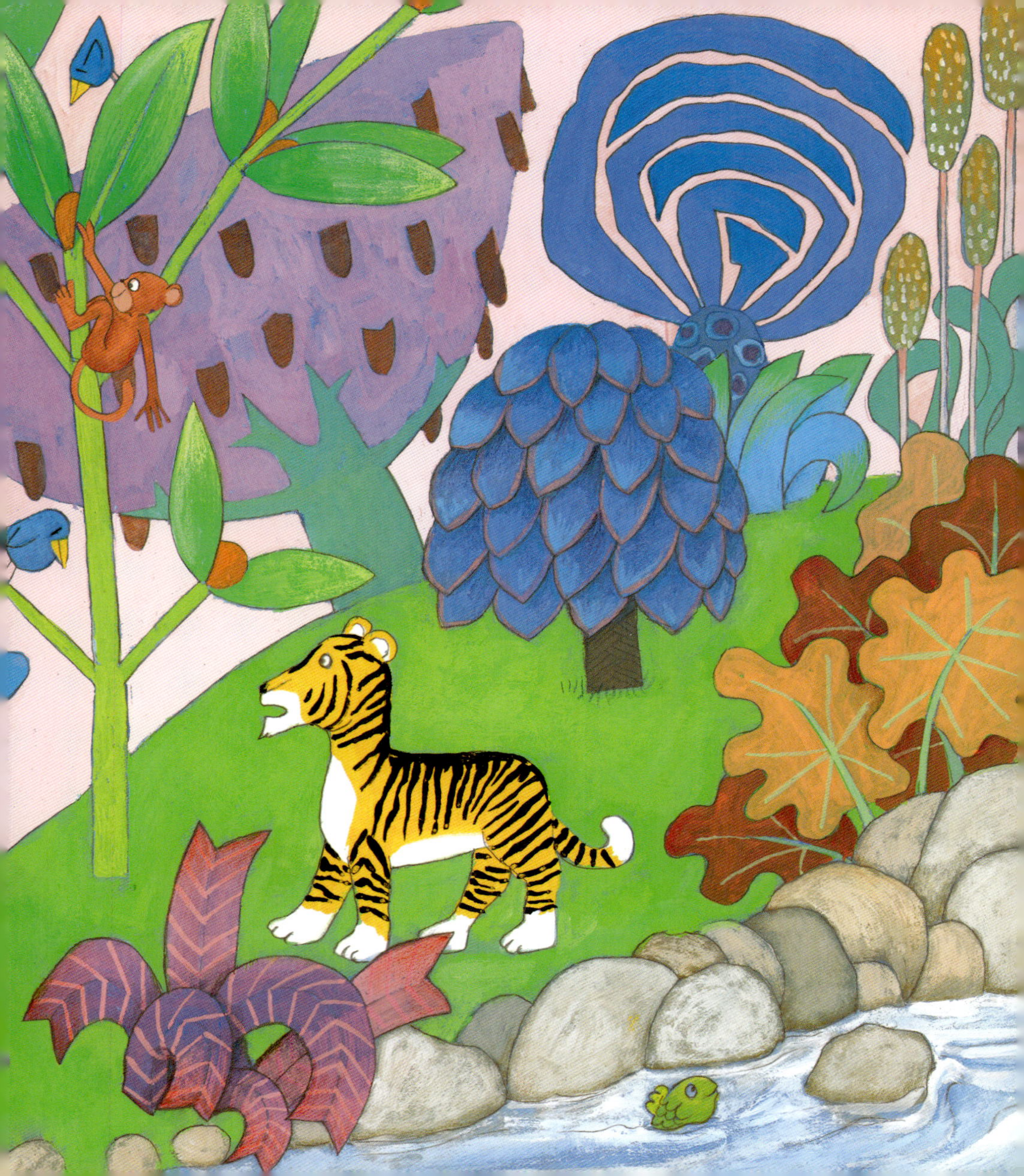

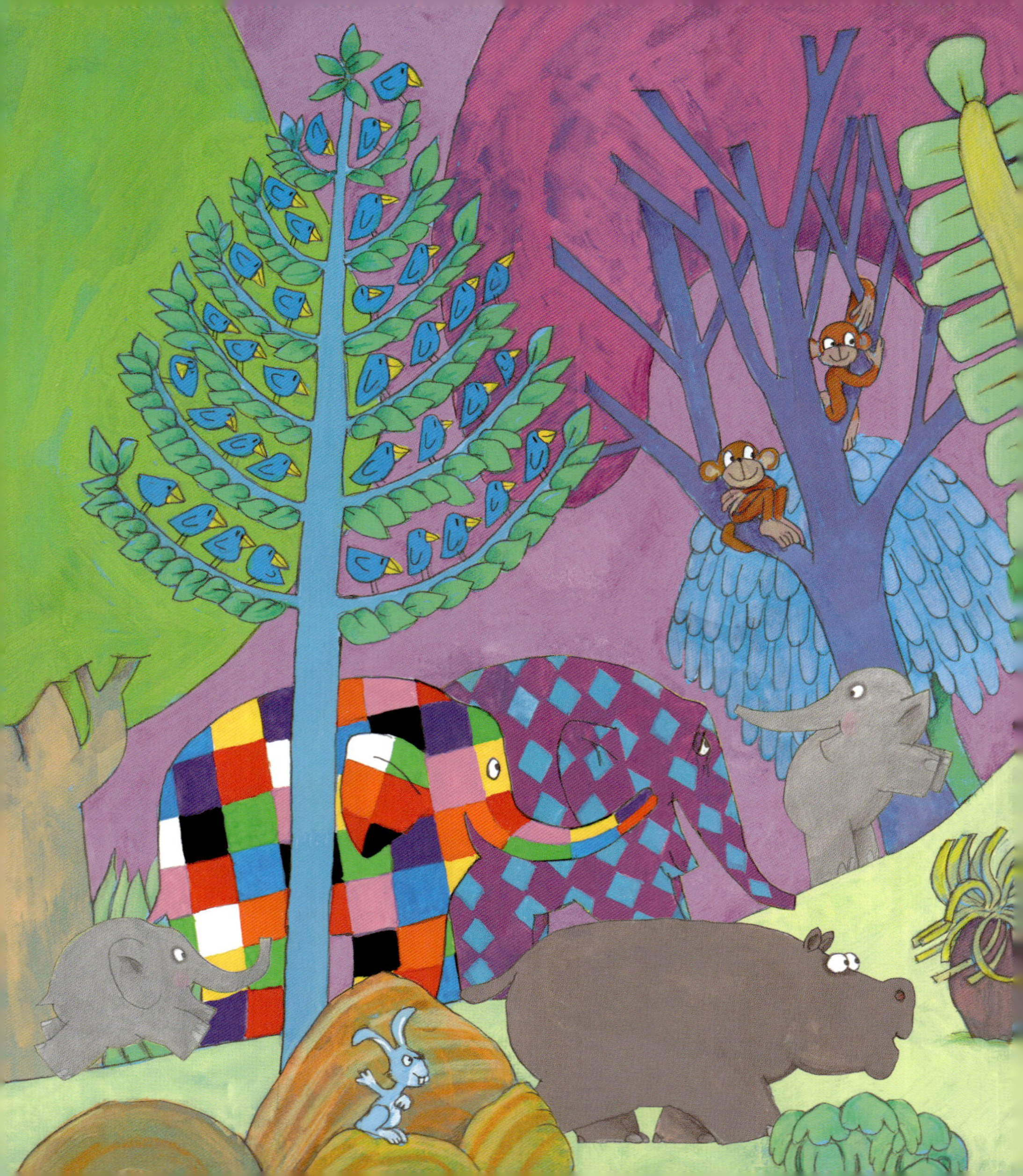

At the end of the walk, everyone had gathered together.

"I'm sorry we couldn't find out how the story goes, Zelda," said Rose. "How will the baby elephants get to sleep now?"

"Oh well, everyone had a lot of good suggestions," Zelda sighed.

"There's an idea," said Elmer, "we can tell a new story together!"

"Once upon a time . . ." he started.

". . . near a beautiful lake," continued Hippo.

". . . there lived a monkey!" said Monkey.

"Don't forget the magic biscuit," said Zelda.

". . . yes, it was magic because it kept disappearing," added Tiger.

"I wonder if it was teatime," said Rose.

"But what happens in the end?"

"Shh," whispered Aunt Zelda.
"They're already asleep!"

2024 IS ELMER'S 35TH BIRTHDAY!

For 35 years, Elmer the patchwork elephant has been helping to spread a message of friendship and compassion to millions of children around the world, encouraging us to celebrate our differences and embrace difference in others.

Happy birthday, Elmer!

DAVID MCKEE
(1935 – 2022)

Across his 60 year career as an author and illustrator, David McKee created many family favourites such as *Not Now, Bernard*, *Mr Benn* and *Elmer the Patchwork Elephant*. His Elmer stories promote inclusivity and friendship, themes that have resonated with millions of children around the world, and will continue to live on for many more generations through his joyful, heartfelt stories.

Discover Elmer's world with over thirty stories and many more exciting adventures to enjoy!

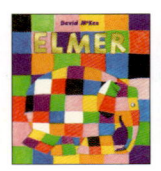

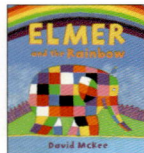

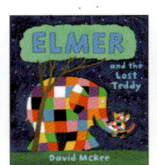

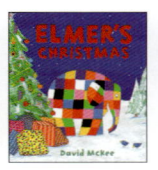

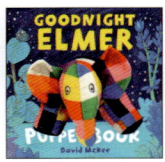

Find out more at www.elmer.co.uk